DOÑA ESMERALDA, WHO ATE EVERYTHING!

For Lola Eleng, who liked to eat! —Melissa

For Mom and Dad —Primo

ISBN 978-1-338-86487-8

Text copyright © 2022 by Melissa de la Cruz. Illustrations copyright © 2022 by Primo Gallanosa. All rights reserved. Published by Orchard Books, an imprint of Scholastic Inc., *Publishers since 1920*. ORCHARD BOOKS and design are registered trademarks of Watts Publishing Group, Ltd., used under license. SCHOLASTIC and associated logos are trademarks and/or registered trademarks of Scholastic Inc.

The publisher does not have any control over and does not assume any responsibility for author or third-party websites or their content.

12 11 10 9 8 7 6 5 4 3 2   22 23 24 25 26 27

Printed in the U.S.A.   40

First Scholastic paperback printing, September 2022

Primo Gallanosa's illustrations were created using digital illustration in Photoshop. The text type was set in Century Schoolbook. The display type is imbroken created by Rae Crawford. This book was art directed by Patti Ann Harris, designed by Rae Crawford, and edited by Liza Baker and Celia Lee.

DOÑA ESMERALDA, WHO ATE EVERYTHING!

By **Melissa de la Cruz**

Illustrated by **Primo Gallanosa**

SCHOLASTIC INC.

ONCE UPON A TIME,

in the middle of a group of seven thousand happy islands named after King Philip of Spain, there lived a lady named Doña Esmeralda. She had a big bouffant hairdo and was much smaller than you.

She was about the size of a toddler, but she was very, very old. Do you know the word *ancient?* It means older than old, and that's how old Doña Esmeralda was.

Doña Esmeralda had a voracious appetite.
That means she was always hungry.
Nothing ever satisfied her.
If she could, she would eat everything in sight.

But because she was small and forgotten, she had to settle for
what she could get.

And that meant leftovers.

Lots and lots of leftovers.

She became especially good at gobbling up what you, and children like you, didn't want to eat.

Doña Esmeralda lived on eating children's uneaten plates and diet soda.

To make it easier, she carried two straws: one for gulping down her diet soda and one to slurp up everything else.

If you didn't like the taste of tofu?
She ate it.

Leftover liver and onions?
She'd suck it up with her straw.

She supped on soggy brussels sprouts and attacked all
the asparagus. She munched on mushy mushrooms and gorged on
gooey grapefruit. She feasted on fresh broccoli and scarfed up
squishy sweet potatoes.

She went to town on tiramisu and zoomed up zucchini bread.
What's tiramisu? Ask your parents. They love it!

(Also, you should really eat your zucchini bread. It's yummy!)
And she gobbled on the giniling.
(Ugh, the giniling. *No one* likes giniling.)

Where did she put it all? She remained smaller than small.
Some said it all went to her hair. She did have very, very big hair.

Naughty children began to notice.

Naughty children learned that all they had to say was, "I don't want to eat this," and Doña Esmeralda would hear them.

She had ears that were very attuned to what children were doing, which means she was very, very, VERY good at hearing.

She would hear them push away from the table.
She would hear the clang of the fork against the plate.
The rustle of a napkin.
The sniff of disdain.
The complaint.
The lament.
The cry.

She would wait until the coast was clear . . . and pounce!

SLURRRRRPPPpp.

She tasted the tofu.
Sucked up the leftover liver
and onions.
Supped on soggy brussels sprouts.
Attacked all the asparagus.
Munched on mushy mushrooms.
Gorged on gooey grapefruit.
Feasted on fresh broccoli.
Scarfed up squishy sweet potatoes.

Went to town on tiramisu.
(You know what that is by now.)

And zoomed up zucchini bread.
(Which is very tasty; you should
not have left it on your plate!)

She even gobbled on the giniling.
(Ugh, the giniling. No one likes
giniling. Except Doña Esmeralda.)
She ate every bit.

YUCK!

No matter where Doña Esmeralda went, she was always hungry, and she was always on the lookout for her next meal.

Until one day, something happened that hadn't happened before.

One day, she heard something she hadn't heard before . . .

She heard the children eating!
Not only eating, but feasting!
Gobbling! Chewing! Slurping!
Munching! Wolfing! Gulping!
Tasting! Licking! Sipping!
Attacking! Gorging! Scarfing!

And laughing!

It was a party. A party with plenty of
food that smelled and looked delicious!

When it was over, there was nothing left on their plates!
Not a crumb.
Not a speck.
Nothing.
Nothing for Doña Esmeralda, who was very, very hungry.

Doña Esmeralda was mad, and HUNGRY!

She was HANGRY!
And she was tired of eating what the children
didn't want to eat.
She was sick of leftovers!
She wanted to eat what the children wanted to eat!

The next day, she followed the children to a picnic by the zoo. This time, she crept out of the shadows, and when the children weren't looking, she ate what they ate. She slurped it up with her straw.

Chicken nuggets.
Hamburgers.
Pizza.

MMMMMMM!

Kare-kare.
Chop suey.
Samosas.

YUMMMMM!

Milkshakes.
Adobo.
Pancit.

NOMMMM!

Lumpia.
Bulgogi.
Tikka masala.

BURP!

The food tasted delicious, and she ate more than she ever ate before. But Doña Esmeralda wasn't satisfied. *Satisfied* means happy, which she wasn't.

She looked around.
What else could she eat?

She took out her straw and just started to SLURRRPPP.

She slurped the plates, the table, the chairs. YUMMY!

She slurped a vine, a bush, and a tree. HE HE!

She slurped up an elephant and a crocodile. CHOMP!

She slurped up a carabao, a monkey-eating eagle, and a giant vegetarian bat. GULP!

Doña Esmeralda still wanted more, so she slurped up the naughty children. **(Boo-hoo!)**

She slurped up the good children. **(Very well!)**

She slurped up their parents, too. **(It's our fault!)**

And that still wasn't enough!

But even Doña Esmeralda bit off more than she could chew when she slurped up ALL THE DIET SODA.

Her tummy began to rumble.

Her bouffant was ready to tumble. And then . . .

BOOM!

Out went the parents.

Out came the good and the naughty children.

Out, out, out went . . .

       the giant vegetarian bat, the monkey-eating eagle, the carabao,

          the crocodile, the elephant,

            the tree, bush, and vine, and

              the chairs, table, and plates!

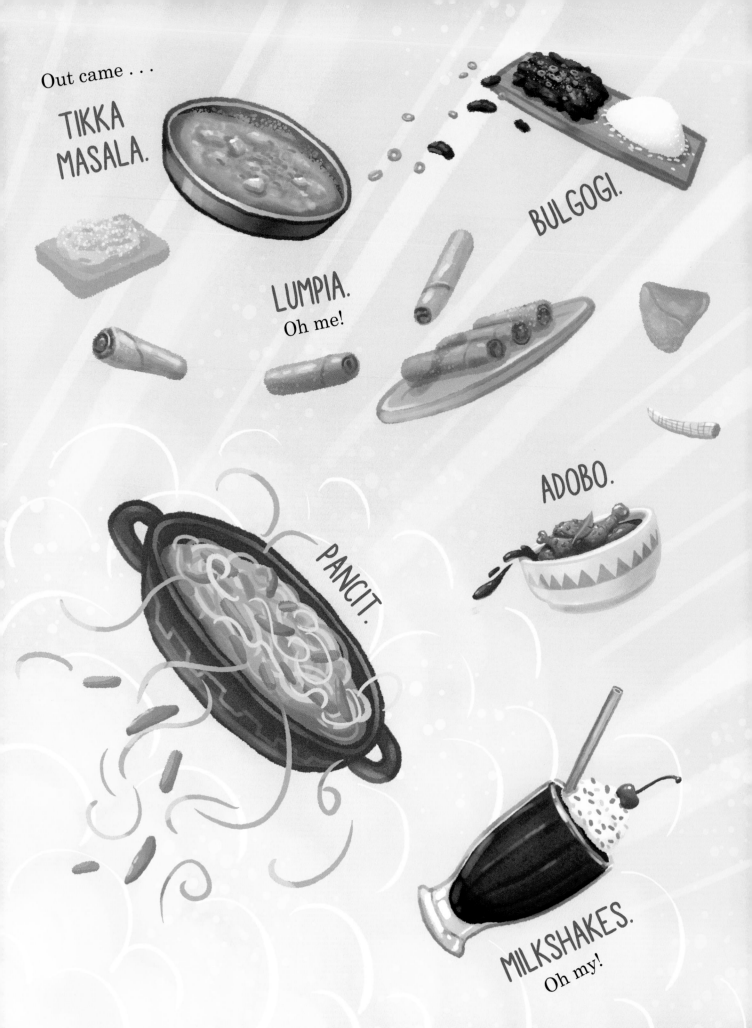

And out, out, out came the leftovers:

Giniling. (Ugh! Giniling.)

Zucchini bread.

Tiramisu.

AYAYAY!

Sweet potatoes.

Broccoli.

Grapefruit.

HOHOHO!

Mushrooms.

Asparagus.

Brussels sprouts.

JEEZ LOUISE!

Liver and onions.

Tofu.

GOLLY GEE!

That was the end of Doña Esmeralda.
The end means,
well, you know what it means.

Ay, patay!

Without Doña Esmeralda, from then on,
all children always ate everything on their plates.

But the naughty ones still try, to this day, to say, "I don't wanna eat this," and they hope that Doña Esmeralda will return with her straw.

Hopefully she does not slurp you up, too.

THE END.

AUTHOR'S NOTE

When I was a kid, my parents gave me a book of Filipino folktales by Nick Joaquin. The story "Lilit Bulilit and the Babe-in-the-Womb," about a little lady with a bouffant hairdo who eats and eats, stayed with me. I remembered the bouffant hairdo, the straw, the explosion, and the string of pearls that were left behind. The story is a take on the Filipino myth of the *aswang* – a vampire-type monster with a narrow and tubular tongue who sucks the lifeblood out of people.

I wanted to pay homage to that story and to all the delicious Filipino foods of my childhood. As well as all the foods I did not like! As a kid, I detested giniling. UGHHH giniling (ground beef), which our cook made every week. I *loathed* it, and I had to eat it. I wish Doña Esmeralda would have come and ate it off my plate. My kid disliked sweet potatoes when she was a babe. I remember her just spitting them out, the orange dribbling down her chin. The more I think on this story now, I realize how subversive it is: In Nick Joaquin's book, Lilit Bulilit is drawn as a Spanish Doña, a Spanish lady, in the style of the colonial elite. It's a sly critique of our history. Filipino humor. Filipino folktales. Filipino genius. Look up the Nick Joaquin stories; they are inspiring.

And because I'm nice, on the next page, there's a recipe of my mom's amazing lumpia. Eat it before Doña Esmeralda does!

—Melissa de la Cruz

FRIED VEGETABLE LUMPIA
WITH PORK AND SHRIMP

Ingredients

1 tbsp cooking oil, plus more as needed
1 onion, chopped
4-5 cloves garlic, minced
3/4 lb. pork, cut into thin strips
Fish sauce to taste (optional)
Salt and pepper to taste
1/2 lb. shrimp, shelled and cut into
small pieces
2 medium carrots, julienned into small strips
1 cup green beans, thinly cut diagonally
1 cup shredded cabbage
2 cups bean sprouts
1 16 oz. package of lumpia or spring roll wrappers

Dipping Sauce

1/3 cup vinegar
1 tsp soy sauce
3 cloves garlic, minced
Salt and pepper to taste

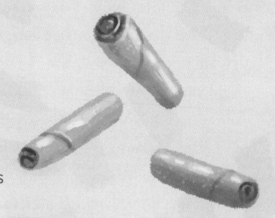

1. Heat 1 tbsp cooking oil in a pan or skillet.
2. Sauté the onion until translucent, then add the minced garlic.
3. Add the pork and sauté until lightly browned. Season with 1 tbsp fish sauce or salt.
4. Add about 1/4 cup of water, cover, and simmer for a few minutes until the pork is tender and the water has evaporated. (If needed, add 1 tbsp cooking oil.) Add the shrimps and cook until pink. Add carrots, green beans, shredded cabbage, and bean sprouts and cook for a few minutes. (Note: Do not overcook vegetables; keep them halfway done.)
5. Season with salt and pepper to taste.
6. Remove from pan, transfer to a colander, and set aside to cool completely before wrapping.
7. Separate each wrapper individually.
8. Spoon the cooled filling onto the wrapper positioned diagonally, with one corner facing you.
9. Fold the sides, tuck both ends inward, and roll tightly into a log.
10. Brush the wrapper's tip with water to seal.
11. Deep-fry until golden and crispy.
12. Mix vinegar dipping sauce ingredients.
Serve with fried lumpias.

Melissa de la Cruz is the #1 *New York Times* bestselling author of many critically acclaimed and award-winning novels for readers of all ages, including her most recent hits: Disney's Descendants series, the Alex & Eliza trilogy, the Queen's Assassin duology, and the Never After series. Melissa grew up in Manila, Philippines, where she happily ate all kinds of yummy food, except the dreaded giniling. She lives in Los Angeles with her family and drinks a lot of Diet Coke.

Primo Gallanosa is an author and illustrator and created the book *Hey, Who Made This Mess?*, and the award-winning children's app called Pocket Worlds. He has lived in Southern California all his life and attended the prestigious art school CalArts. When Primo isn't drawing, you can find him playing video games, reading a book, or surfing. He lives in Los Angeles with his wife, Marie Lu, and two adorable pups.